La Ronde

Colin Fisher

La Ronde
by Colin Fisher
ISBN: 978-1-908125-85-9

Cover Art by David Rix

Publication Date: May 2020

La Ronde

Brokenness can be its own perfection. The caterpillar dissolves within its pupa to give life to the butterfly. Granite is worn by the strife of years into glittering mica. The sculptor's hammer destroys a marble block to create a masterpiece. And at its most fundamental, the living, breathing body fades into earth, its sole purpose to give new life, new growth. Everything that is made is something else broken.

Death too has something of the malady of perfection, for what is death if not life broken? All my ancestors are dead, yet have attained their own exquisite form that far outlasts their earthly raiment. My sister and I are the sole living recipients of the Laronde genes. The dead outnumber the living, and art outnumbers us all.

You will, of course, have already noted the novelty of our own humble addition to the Laronde name. Yes, my sister and I are unique – if I may be granted the indulgence of allowing two within the definition rather than one – in that not only are we the first twins ever to grace the family line, but also, indeed, ours is the only generation represented by more than a single individual. In no other time or place that our family has crafted, laboured, performed or excelled, has any member ever – and I say this not lightly since the great library at Vistagnue can trace our history from the earliest dynasties of the lost Etruscan world from which we descend – produced more than a single offspring, one only, sufficient to carry our line into each fresh century. Perhaps it was wrong – it was certainly *naïf* – but the love our father felt for his muse, the degree to which she inspired and tormented him, was so extreme in its vicissitudes, so all-encompassing, that he knew an extreme gesture of creation was the only true response he could offer. An *opus magnifique.* He embraced her as he embraced the extravagance of his art, with all its agony and triumph, and, if his ancestors would have disapproved, why then at least he fulfilled his genius and talent in this one triumphant failing.

The above is, of course, supposition. Although both he and our mother live on in us, I never knew my father beyond the likeness he left behind, and whilst at times of reflection, I like to imagine his soul's brush has laid its wash within us, it is difficult to divine his exact purpose, or the motivations that led him to defy such a weight of tradition. Often I have gazed upon his visage, at the moods the stone has captured, and I have caught myself with such questions upon my lips. And I wonder if all who stood there before me have pondered such unanswerable questions. If not all were orphans at the beginning, all became so as death and art wove its tapestry upon them.

How may I describe the place in which Gabrielle and myself drew our first breath? It is *une merveille*, a wonder beyond human comprehension, to which all our muses, should they prove themselves to be worthy of the name, are invited, so that they may ponder the miracle of which they are part. I have stood beneath the Great Dome, every inch of which is covered by a tumult of celestial beings caparisoned in rich golds and purples and blues, and known that were they living gods, every figure would testify to the masterwork that is La Ronde. It is, of course, from this great room and its singular work, that we are named. The room is a vast organism (yes, truly, for such a masterpiece of colour and light and movement can only be understood in the context of a living thing), a circle as its name implies, and it is the greatest work of artistic genius that exists in the world, or has ever existed, beyond Donatello, Michelangelo, beyond all the nameless prodigies of vanished centuries. Even Pheidias, although it is said of him that when Vesnia Losnai (one of our earliest foremothers, and a peerless worker of bronze and terracotta) visited his studio at Olympia, she was so moved by his metalwork that she declared him worthy of his own place in La

Ronde. Indeed, she commissioned from him the twin statues of chryselephantine that now stand inside the leaving doors.

Imagine a frieze that encompasses the entire circumference of the room, a span of four hundred and seventy feet. This frieze is a procession of ancestors, each a perfect sculpt in the purest of marbles, caught in the moment of the greatest expression of their art, whichever endeavour that represents. Some are carving, some are painting. Some breathe life into the hardest of granites, others present a miracle of pigment, bronze, stone, cloth or even music. Yet everywhere there is art, the incomparable genius that is our birthright. And unlike the poor degraded frieze that is all that remains of Pheidias' genius upon the Parthenon, La Ronde retains its riot of colours – aquamarine, scarlet, saffron, cerise, azure – in truth, more hues than the mortal eye can recognise. Every colour is as pristine as the day it was created, so that the blush upon the cheeks of our earliest ancestors are no less vivid than that upon our father's own likeness. And beyond his outstretched arms, caught in the act of bringing Gabrielle and myself into existence, the frieze stretches on blankly, ready to receive the likeness of generations of Laronde yet unborn, until the circle is complete, returning to the far doors through which we never venture, and from which our art began. Unlike the near doors, which lead through subterranean passageways to our own workshops, and which are bound with intricate bands of beaten gold and the ivory of long-extinct creatures, embossed with fabulous designs and a king's ransom in jewels, they are plain bronze, unadorned, cold, and reflect only the rare and pale light of the room's illumination. Only the twin statues of Feronia and Vertumnus, gods of fire, passion and death, commissioned by Vesnia, compete with their blind, unswerving presence.

It is here that I have often come to stand before my father's upturned face, streaked with tears of stone as translucent and piteous as my own, and seen how he gazes back at his father, and his father's father, and so on into the deeps of time, men and women of one name and destiny, and have wondered why he defied them all, ordaining that we two should have, not the serenity nor single-mindedness which was the birthright of every one of our ancestors, but conflict, competition, the criticism of siblings. The doubt that stills our hand, the torment of our kinship.

I do not want to give the impression that this is something I dwell on inordinately. It is, rather, something I feel to be a consequence of my sister's reluctance to speculate upon the underlying rationale of our existence. When we were young, finding our way in the world, inquisitive and impulsive as is the nature of children, I asked her once if she supposed our father, being of a rebellious nature, had intended that we should come into this world as living symbols of his ceaseless disregard for strictures and rules, his courting of opprobrium, the same defiance of tradition and culture witnessed in his art. If, as I have suggested, his passion for our mother was so extreme and encompassing that we could be the only honest and true representation of this love, the ultimate expression of his genius. She would pause in her practice, touch her ivory fingers to the smooth curve of a sculpture's lips, or the modesty implicit in a portrait's lowered glance, and without looking at me she would smile sadly, and say "Oh *Sébastien*, how romantic you are! How *passionné!* Have you not considered, rather, the tension in art, the conflict implicit in creation? The artist must destroy. It is in our nature. This block of marble, fashioned in the Earth's titanic embrace, must be deformed to shape the lineaments of even the humblest beauty. This canvas, innocent in emptiness, must be contained within a grave of oils that smother its fragile purity. You suppose we represent the uncontainable artifice in our father's love, yet it would serve you better to consider rather the limitless selfishness of the creative flame. We are the highest expression of that flame, *'the fire for which all thirst'* as our beloved Shelley puts it, and in us our father sought to depict that impulse of destruction, that endless conflict of the abstract muse. We exist to create, and yet, in creation we destroy. Nature is immolated in the name of Art. And, as we know, we cannot both be so perpetuated. The sculptor's knife can immortalise only one. There will be war in heaven, and we shall burn with Lucifer's flame, and neither love nor art will heed the loser's heart.' And she turned to me then, and placed her lips beside my ear, and whispered, 'I will exist, and my art shall exist, and I will be complete within it. Our father's bequest was war, not peace." And then she laughed, and kissed me on the cheek, and turned back to her blades and punches, and the chisels that enticed the hidden shapes from within eternal stone.

Mine had been a difficult birth. Gabrielle was the elder by a day; she had emerged with ease, our mother almost taken by surprise and thus delivering her with little more than a scant few hours of gasps and groans amid the short bursts of intense pain that signified my sister's arrival. I was a wholly different matter – our mother exhausted, her reserves of strength and energy depleted as she strained and cried out in her confinement. My sister watched silently as our mother and father, each with their unique contribution, laboured to bring forth my troubled soul to the light of day. The hours slipped into night as he struggled with the intensity of birth, as mother twisted and strained to usher me into the world wreathed in blood, anointed by her sacrifice and his desire. Never was such a life conceived. One birth, one giving of life to another, was arduous enough, would wrench body and soul as an ocean storm wrenches timber and sail from a stately galleon, but two? That was folly, magnificent folly that had never been attempted in our family; the iron and fire of our vision, our blood, more than enough to vanquish the scions of men even with a single progeny, and as our mother's strength waned in exhaustion and agony, our father too struggled amid the affirmation to urge her soul's fire to one final flare. They both died, of course, our mother and our father, and as I took my first breath my sister held me in the wreckage of their flesh, blood the first pigment we knew.

Thus were we orphaned from the moment of our creation; as a celestial conflagration gives birth to new stars within the whirling tumults of matter's divine furnace, atoms ascending to the godhood of each incipient sphere in ceaseless, primordial fury, so Gabrielle and I were born from our parents' ardour but left them behind to forge our own path through a firmament of passion, art and beauty. And what is left of such a furnace but a perfection that has drawn all else in upon itself, devouring the elements it must have to exist, leaving them vanquished? So it was with us. All was gone, yet we shone brighter for that sacrifice. That is not to say that we should be pitied, for self-reliance, or, rather reliance on each other, was in our nature. We may not have had our father or mother to provide for our necessities, to tutor us and demonstrate our place in the great work of life, but that merely allowed our own talents to flourish, our own perceptions and vision to evolve in the immaculate heat of our creativity and skill.

We learned our craft together, side by side, the first generation in our family to be of one mind, but two flesh.

When I was young I would lie upon the floor of our gilded chapel, gazing for hours at the painted ceiling that arched above me, its perfect cerulean darkening to the deep blues and blacks of the starry firmament, veins of gold amongst the plaster as immaculate as the day they were laid. I imagined God as artist, stars as flecks of paint upon the canvas of Creation, adding or subtracting just the right scarlet and vermillion to coax His vision into existence, and I would imagine artist as God; creator, possessor and demiurge, magician and performer, entrancing all, irresistible sculptor of indivisible destinies. I imagined myself as God, and my sister as Goddess, and wondered if such poetry and beauty as we two shaped existed in the World's beginning, when the gods moulded stone and sea, when perilous mortal clay took shape by primordial waters, and the *logos* ran like blood through Earth's veins. Was that our purpose? To descend upon the mortal realm with the undiminished Word echoing between our hands? Did the gods possess such power of life as we two, our whims the beautiful engine of a privileged birth? My sister thought so. "In us, Creation lives on," she would say, gesturing with a curved knife, "What a gift is in this blade, this brush. Our birthright, through all the centuries of our forefathers. Why else do we exist but to create and destroy at the gesture of this palette, this exquisite mortality?" I could never disagree, for together we wove such a seduction of form and colour among our marble colonnades and dusty halls that all those who saw them, or attended our occasional *salons*, were entranced.

Despite our closeness, Gabrielle was never jealous of my loves, my pursuits amorous or intellectual. She had more than enough beauty and grace to attract any suitor she desired, without desiring mine. Yet, somehow, she acquired them, effortlessly. Time and again, those I desired became her muses, her inspiration. I can say, without false modesty, that I was her equal for beauty, for poise and *élan*, yet repeatedly they would drift from me, become no more than a half-drawn outline upon an empty canvas, as if it were my sister's art alone could give them life, colour, substance. She did not do this deliberately, I do not believe. She had a natural air of mystery, of elusiveness, that wayward souls, those themselves adrift on the idle breezes of life's chance, found irresistible. My own temperament leaned more toward the studious, the contemplative (morose, as Gabrielle termed it), which, although initially attractive, seemed at length to repel my muses into my sister's carefree embrace, fuelling her endless and inventive portraits, studies, sculptures and sketches. The lightest pressure of her thumbs on clay, her brush dancing on canvas, would capture them, their solitude, their gaiety, their fragility and hopelessness, and they would be entranced. Where I might take a month to trace the curve of a sensuous lip or arching brow, my sister would define, draw, sculpt an entire weaving, dancing naiad of erotic grace. Her talents, to which mine should have been equal, flowered as the heart-shaped petals of the golden *ficaire* spread and flower beneath the Mediterranean sun, while mine, I was convinced, began to atrophy and wither as the years passed. That this was her design, that even then she was looking to the day when she would complete the Great Work in my stead, I did not want to believe. Indeed, I do not believe even now that she regarded her place in our family line as inevitable, or something to be brought to a swift conclusion. I believe it was not until she saw the effect that her successes, conscious or unconscious, had on my own creativity, that such a conceit began to take hold. And thus, even as my art began to turn in upon itself, and the lustre and promise of my early masterpieces went unfulfilled, did I fail to perceive the folly of my own indulgence.

Katya was my muse before she turned to Gabrielle. Of course, it is sometimes difficult to remember such things accurately, or in the order in which they actually occurred. And if this is not true, should you forgive me? No, for then this recollection is itself art. The artist must never request forgiveness. Art is like dreaming. When we wake, we are a different person. Lifetimes of certainties are belied by the stroke of a brush, the revelation of a hidden design. Yet I am as certain as it may be.

There came, one day, a turning point. Certainly for me, and perhaps also for my sister. At the time neither of us acknowledged this as anything other than the latest in an escalating series of ill-tempered *contretemps* that had seen us hold separate, rival, *expositions* for the elite of the Vaucluse art world, and which I felt confident would eventually attain an armistice in a new joint venture or collaboration. With the benefit of hindsight (ironic, in the circumstance) I might now pinpoint this as something different. The time, perhaps, when we attained a degree of . . . adulthood? Maturity? At least, if not that, a recognition that our fates, inextricable as they seemed to be, would one day take the path that our own blazing Lucifer, our mad, passionate, reckless father, had ordained for us.

I had crossed words with Gabrielle that day. She had arisen from her *toilette* to find me struggling with the crossed muscles in my *Death of Alexander*. I had undertaken a certain artistic license, and had our hero tormented by the fever that claimed him, raised upon one arm and with the other reaching out for the vision that his madness drew – of a world conquered by his armies; citadels and kings beyond the Indus prostrate at his feet. His arm knotted, his fingers clutched, even as his weakness robbed him of triumph and he fell back upon the pillows. For some reason, I struggled with the forearm. This was key to the entire figure, twisting muscles that must convey his longing, the entirety of the conqueror's torment and pathos. Gabrielle circled me, head tilted, as I struggled, chisel in hand, sweating like my stricken hero to impart motion and truth to his agony. She stood for a moment by his upraised arm, touching it lightly with her perfect pale hands. "It is inhuman," she pronounced at length. "You have raised the *flexor radialis* too much. Here. It would cut across the plane of the *brachioradialis*. No man, even in their extremity, could adopt such a shape. Desire is in the fingers, not the arms." She was right, but I was furious. I had known for a week that my Alexander was fit only for the hammer. Yet my stubbornness had kept me at him. Perhaps I saw something of my own longing in his madness for completion. "Oh, it is you who are inhuman!" I cried, flinging my chisel at her. With a laugh, she spun away, her gown awhirl with motes of marble dancing in the lamplight. I seethed as I heard her the light slap of her bare feet receding on the tessellated floor.

I could do no more work that day, so I decided to lose myself in the human tide that flowed about the cafes and squares of the old town. The glamour of the peacock tide, its joy, despair and yearning. I remember ascending from the Gallery, its litany of changing fashions a constant amusement to me, and exiting onto the *Rue Racine* with the scent of fish and spiced meats in my nostrils. The Turkish cafe on the corner was rich with coffee and smoke, and an autumn chill drove early evening passers-by inside. I ignored its blandishments, thinking instead that the cafes by *Rue des Teinturiers* might more readily suit my mood.

Rain fell in glittering spikes. The Sorgue was alive with faces, each reflection in its limpid surface a portrait of its own devising, sketches of laughter and hunger and those poisoned shafts of flattery that were the emblems of the city's ceaseless dissertation. Night wove lustrous images from the sparks of their desire, and they in turn were reflected in the dark water, flickering and gesticulating as if they were drowning, which they were.

I loved them all, at different times and for different purposes. Art knows no prejudice, owes fealty to none but Truth. I could not say some there were ugly, for their scowls and brutish mien conjured Saturn, choking down his sons in paroxysms of fear. The arrogance of others begat Caesar, triumph cowed by old men. Inspiration for myself and Gabrielle lurked in the most improbable of guises. And for those few truly beautiful, who might walk among gods and not raise hackles at their daring, there was the immortality of marble, of weeks and months of tears and exultation in the service of their gift and ours.

All knew me. They stood beneath awnings and called good-naturedly, gesturing for me to come out of the rain and join them for a bitter *izarra* or glass of *Viognier*. *Sébastien*, they called, *venez ici! Come here! Bring us some of that famous Auvergne wit!* But they also knew that as often as I would laugh gaily, or regale them with tales of the vulgarity of the rich, I would remain quiet and pensive, and regard them with a morose detachment in my olive eyes. For this reason, more called for my sister, asked where Gabrielle might be, surely not working on such a night of song and drink. Often they would embrace me, or put their arms around my shoulders, and with a conspiratorial wink ask for *la déesse* – the goddess. For Gabrielle never scowled, and a smile was ever about her sensuous lips, and her eyes were twin fires of passion while her fierce intelligence fuelled two or three conversations at once, on art, on history, politics, literature, never once faltering as she flitted between the mesmerised flocks of twittering, doomed sycophants. And on this night of all nights, when my Alexander stretched out his impossible arm to my hubris and failure, and my sister's mocking laughter ran like broken trails of quicksilver in and out of my thoughts, on this night their good-natured calls and entreaties merely layered my misery with the drab leavening of despair.

I could not settle. I nodded to my interrogators but hurried on past the open bars, the humanity that clustered beneath the canal lamps. Hunched,

I sought the isolation of the martyr, to drench my despair amid the hammering rain.

I didn't see her. At that moment I would have failed to see an angel of God had one chosen to descend like Michael before Joshua and upbraid me for my vanity. And an angel she seemed, a shining vessel forged in Heaven and decanted to an earthly realm made leaden by her presence. Such was Katya.

I had crossed the river, in the scant hope that I could drink myself to oblivion without being recognised, and an hour past dusk saw me brooding at a pavement café beneath the shadow of Fort Saint-Andre. High above, clouds had dispersed before the mistral's touch, and moonlight now reflected from the sheen of damp cobbles along the *Rue de la République*. I was sunk in misery, and had determined not only to break my *Alexander* before morning, but to destroy also all the studies and sketches completed in preparation. Perhaps my expression drove away those who would accost me for I was neither hailed nor challenged as I sat, glowering, glass in hand, beneath an awning that shed its last drops of rain before my feet. My hair hung in drying strands, like a clutch of weeds across the face of a drowned man.

"*Monsieur.*" I did not hear her, and she repeated herself. "*Monsieur?* You are the artist, Laronde?"

I roused myself from my reverie. "My sister is the *artist* Laronde," I sneered, "I am merely the *journeyman* Laronde. *Le apprenti* Laronde." I turned, and the sneer died on my face.

She stood in the doorway, a light above tinting her dark hair with a gold that seemed to me a prophetic spark, heaven's kindling setting flames upon her brow. Her eyes were grey, smoky with an opaque amusement that also contoured her lips into a carefree smile. Her cheeks were high, smoother and paler than the marble of Carrara. Her nose, small but straight and purposeful leant her an air of determination, and a scattering of freckles turned her perfection into humanity. She seemed joyful, without guile, as if chancing upon me in the rain-washed streets beneath the Castle's shadow was a fortune greater than her heart could accommodate. She wore an afternoon dress of white satin, heedless of the sodden folds around her ankles, and her hands bunched in the silken tassels of her taffeta jacket. An umbrella, hung in the crook of one arm, showed no sign of having been unfurled.

"*Mademoiselle,*" I stammered, rising, "forgive my rudeness . . . I had not expected . . ."

She laughed. "Rudeness? I had expected no less. Indeed I had expected more from *le magnifique artiste* Sébastien Laronde. As capricious as he is talented, or so they say."

"Is that what they say?"

"There are only two artists worthy of the name in this city." She tipped her nose, and affected the tone of condescension displayed by Vauxcelles and his ilk. "And the name is *Laronde*. For the earth – strength, power, the beauty of stone – Laronde *frère*. For the air – passion, delicacy, the boundless firmament of the canvas – Laronde *soeur*. The one mercurial, capricious, exacting, the other joyful, radiant, carefree."

It was true. In us, the energies and talents of the Laronde family had divided like the cell that made us twins. We were equally talented (or had been), but our temperaments urged us upon different paths. And yet, to take Gabrielle no further than the face she chose to present to the world was to mistake her appetites, her hunger. No one who had seen her rage upon a misapplied brushstroke, or the arm of a dancing figure raised a millimetre too high, would believe her incapable of fury or destruction. She was at least my equal in that.

"I hope I do not offend?" She tilted her head, and her hair tumbled in darkness and light around her throat. I watched it, captivated, and it was all I could do to gesture to the seat beside me, in wonder that such a creature had chosen to descend to this humble roadside café.

Her father had been a cavalry officer in the Imperial Russian Army. Wounded in the liberation of the Balkans from the Ottoman (a subject captured in my *Last Day at Shipka*), he had never recovered, and died when she was still a child. She had two brothers. The elder had followed her father into the cavalry, the younger absconded with the family fortune and bestowed it upon a dancer in Naples. Already a noted beauty, Katya was married at eighteen to an ancient Hungarian aristocrat who promised to rescue the family from penury, and made good on his word by falling from his horse in a drunken stupor less than a month after the wedding, leaving Katya mistress of a comfortable stipend from estates on the Danube. Preferring the fashionable ambience, sun and artistry of the Vaucluse to the dark hills of their Transdanubian foster home, she settled with her mother in a moderately luxurious villa north of the Rhone, and embraced all that the south had to offer.

I listened to Katya far into the night, as the clouds drew south and the summer wind moved her hair about her face. When the exasperated *patron* finally threw us out an hour past closing time, we walked beneath the sycamores on the *Rue Montee du Fort,* and when the shadows of the white stone walls gave way to the brick and plaster of the lower town, I walked her back to her *hôtel.* While her lips moved, it was her eyes that told her story. I longed to sketch her, to find her form in clay, to strip her gown and paint her flawless skin, the gestures with which she erased my bitterness. I would mould the soft sweep of her back from her slender shoulders to the curve of her thighs, and I would cast her breasts full under the most luminous moonlight sheen. All these things I promised myself while still her eyes – wide with laughter, dark with remembered loss, lowered with concealment and the illusion of modesty – held my gaze and promised me that she would be my muse.

I did not return to our house that night, or the next, preferring instead the anonymity of a *pension*. Days drew into weeks, and autumn coloured the streets with reds and burning gold. My absence would elicit no reaction from Gabrielle. We were often gone for days at a time, either through amorous pursuits, or seeking inspiration in the towns and villages about the city. She would believe that I sulked, and knew from experience that I would return with my humour restored, mollified by whichever pursuit I had chosen to immerse myself in, captive to some fresh enthusiasm.

Each day I met Katya. I took her to the galleries, to the *théâtre*, to restaurants, to street performances, to lectures and museums. Through all, I ached to draw her. To bring her vibrancy, her colour, to a more permanent form of life. To transcend the limitations of her mortal frame and capture that beauty, that living artistry in oil, in clay, in smooth Carrera marble. I needed to expose her to the eternal truth of art. It was a fever. When I stood in her presence, it burned my heart, seared my fingers, my eyes, quickened my breath and tightened my stomach to a knot of butterflies. I longed to pose her, and look deep into the wells of her untrammelled soul.

Naturally she urged me, pleaded. How could she not? She knew my reputation, and having found me, needed me to elevate her to immortality. So why did I not abandon my *pension*, return with her to our *palais d'art* beneath the *Place de l'Horloge,* to the grand chapel, to the chambers and galleries hung with the masterworks of a hundred generations of Laronde, to my studio? Something held me back, always. Some caution, some fear. Gabrielle. I had to have Katya, she had to speak to my art, could do so in a manner none had before, but would she stay true to me? Or would my sister's vision, its grace, perfection and delicacy, steal her away to those rooms where stood the fruits of Gabrielle's incomparable eye, as it had so many others before. No, that I would not risk.

It was four weeks before I saw Gabrielle. She sat beneath a plane tree on the *Rue de la République.* She was alone, sipping coffee, reading one of the execrable pulp novels she was addicted to. The shadows of broad leaves moved across her face. Of course, she knew I was there, as I did her – those who share one blood are often of the same mind – and I saw her push her golden hair (inherited from our mother) away from her face and cast her eyes around the square. I took Katya's hand to hurry her away, but she tugged me back, bending to examine a fabric from a street vendor, and I felt Gabrielle's eyes upon us.

I knew precisely what expression she had adopted. It would be that look of superior amusement that was so often about her lips. Ah! She would exclaim, here comes *Sébastien* with his latest *divertissement*! *Quel amusant!* How he runs from his failures, how he sulks. Yes, there had been occasions when I had done just such. When an unfair review or casual *salon* witticism had propelled me, furious, to the bars and clubs of the Sorgue, or to less salubrious pursuits until, sated, I returned at last to my sculpts and canvasses. But this was different. Katya was different. Even here, amid the cobbles and majesty of the old town, where life and colour and laughter were at their gayest, Katya shone like a seam of gold in a coalmine, and the vendors and the musicians and the *artist pavé* and all to whom she turned the flame of her indulgence were entranced. And I knew that Gabrielle would be too, and I was determined that I, and I alone, would be first to capture that transient perfection and usher it into eternity.

I was compelled. I knew what I had to do even as I felt Gabrielle's smile broaden. As Katya crouched, running a square of Charmeuse silk through her fingers, I seized her by the arm. She looked up, eyes widening, and uttered a murmured apology to the crestfallen vendor as I pulled her across the square.

"Sébastien," she gasped, "what is it? What is the matter?"

"It is today." I spun her to face me, seized her hands in mine, "Today we begin! Now we begin!"

And with that I ran, hand in hand with my Russian goddess, past the cafes and market stalls, past the lunatic Gothic extravagance of the Papal palace, past the galleries where hung the inconsequentialities of my former art. All of which I would surpass.

The entrance to our home was off the *Place de l'Horloge*. An unassuming pair of doors, blue paint flaking now in the Vaucluse sun, opened into a modest hallway. Stairs ascended to rarely used apartments, furniture shrouded in dust cloths, but I tugged Katya further into the building, further into the marvels of our genius. The narrow hall ran the length of the building. Here there were galleries, storerooms, and studios. Here the supplies were delivered, rooms after rooms of canvas, clay, brushes, stone of every texture and hue. Then we descended the great sweeping stair that turned like a corkscrew into the earth. Katya marvelled at the statues, exquisite in their finery, at the paintings whose genius belied their mundane surroundings. A plain doorway opened onto a room that held a bronze horse, rearing at a dragon's lash, its mounted knight thrusting a golden spear at the serpent's belly. There, leaning against a wall, a stack of canvases, half-finished, showed face after face of such delicacy and beauty they might have gathered for a clave of angels. Down the staircase we went, past alcoves of marble busts, the histories of kings and princes and forgotten potentates. We descended past the gothic labour of master masons, through long-forgotten vaults, and pillars wreathed in the likeness of leaves and branches. All basked in the glory of Laronde art. Katya marvelled at the light, spheres of golden flame that burned without smoke or flicker, and yet which never diminished. Creations of my ancestors, their secrets were lost and neither Gabrielle nor myself gave them any thought beyond our gratitude at the pure illumination they bestowed.

At last we reached the cool, locked chambers of our subterranean chateâu. Here our studios filled room after room with blank canvases, clay, stone, all transported through the ingenious mechanism of shafts and pulleys developed over centuries. Here, too, the Great Work stood, La Ronde, our gift to humanity and the divine art it inspired. One day I would show this to Katya, should my art prove the equal of her beauty.

But for now, I needed to sketch, to draw and paint the devices of her soul, the frame of her pale flesh. I offered her refreshment, and as I posed her she spoke of the ageless wonder about us. "So much genius! And yet, you prove yourself worthy of it again and again! How does it not . . . intimidate your own talents?"

"It is our birthright," I offered, "but we must take care that it does not suffocate us. We stand on an edifice carved from the immensity of human truth. It is *magnifique,* and we honour it, but each generation must find its own truth, or the

28

Laronde name stands for nothing. We cannot, we *must not* stand for stagnation. Here," and I moved her arm so that the crystal goblet she clutched was supported by the fingers of her left hand. I knew the weight would otherwise prove onerous.

Her lips curved in a smile. The skin at the corner of her eyes crinkled. "From what I hear, there is no danger of stagnation. Your *Vision of Bernadette* caused a stir as far as London last season."

My brows creased in the tiniest of frowns. "Please remain still." I made an adjustment, dusting my fingers across the charcoal. Then I waved my hand. "Few embrace change. The more elevated one becomes, the greater the height from which one can look down." I raised my shoulders, and let them fall. "Taste is ephemeral, genius immortal. Gabrielle and I care nothing for the concerns of the petty. Only our art survives."

"Critics are petty?" Her eyes widened with mock innocence. "Yet you court their approval."

"Humanity is petty." I nodded, satisfied with my alteration. The sketch did not need the detail of expression, but the angle of the head wanted fealty to her gentle mocking. "But you mistake our intent," I continued, "we must have a voice, but we do not need ears for their opinions, nor eyes to read them. Our art is a gift. If you give someone a gift, or a bounty to improve their lives, do you care to what use it is put?"

"I might, if I thought it squandered. I might not wish to do so again, in another circumstance."

I changed pencils. I wanted the detail of her light dress. "Then your gift has a condition, and thus, it is not a gift it is a bribe. To encourage a pattern of behaviour of which you approve."

Again her lips curved. "Which seems prudent, if only to avoid . . ." The furrow in her brows deepened, "čuvstvo razočarovanija? I can't think of the words."

"A sense of disappointment," Gabrielle said from the doorway.

Inwardly, I cursed, yet allowed no trace of irritation to cross my face. I had hoped my sister would be occupied in the square for hours yet. "Katya Savaryn, Gabrielle Laronde." I raised my finger, "Ah, do not rise. The courtesy is unnecessary, I assure you."

"*Mademoiselle*," Katya made the slightest inclination of her head. "It is my honour."

"The honour is ours." I heard Gabrielle's light step as she crossed the room to inspect my work. "You bestow upon us the gift of your beauty. We shall not disappoint you in the use to which is it put, I assure you."

"How long have you been here?" Frustrated, I placed my sketchpad on the easel. Even as I spoke I was considering how I might arrange the background.

"Long enough." Her perfume – she was an advocate of the new and had been trying *Fleurs d'Espagne* for the last eighteen months – was a heady assault on my senses. A smell of orange and jasmine filled the air. I felt her light touch on my shoulders.

"I'm busy," I said

"I am enchanted to meet you." Pointedly, she ignored me. "I have heard so much about you."

"You have heard nothing about her." I was exasperated. "How could you? I haven't seen you for a month."

She waved her hand. "The *salons*, the clubs. They tell me all I need. *Sébastien Laronde, he has a new obsession. A fierce Ukrainian beauty. Her wit, her intelligence. He is smitten.*" Gabrielle looked over the easel at Katya. "There is a new star in our little firmament."

With that Gabrielle kissed me lightly on the cheek, and danced away. In the doorway she paused, and looked again to Katya. "Yet it is to my brother's firmament that you must cling. He is *un génie.* He will make such a fire of your illumination. In oils, in marble, in bronze. There is not a critic in Vaucluse who will not prostrate themselves before their beauty. Whatever is his delight! He will make such a worship of this temple of your spirit that you will wonder at the passion of it."

Katya's eyes sparkled, and she inclined her head. "You are too kind, *Mademoiselle Laronde.* Yet it is an honour in turn to witness the astonishing beauty of your home, of your art. *C'est une merveille.*"

"A marvel?" A smile played about Gabrielle's lips. "It is. Although, you have not yet seen all that is truly marvellous."

I shot her a look. I did not want to reveal all, yet, nor to overwhelm Katya – or, even worse, inure her – to the wonders she had yet to be a part of. If I showed her La Ronde before she was ready, I feared her natural beauty would be inhibited by the magnificence about her. It was something I yearned to share with her, but it must only come when she might rise to the challenge it posed, not be eclipsed.

Gabrielle had lost none of her delight in taunting me. "We labour, each in our own way, our own Truth. All of this –" and her gesture took in both my studio and the hallways beyond, "is but *une petite partie* of the greater whole. The Great Work. Would you not say, *Sébastien?*"

"Do you have no work of your own to attend, *ma sœur bienaimée?* You have a private view soon, do you not?"

Her smile broadened. "Ah yes! Thank you for reminding me. I have been neglectful. *Mademoiselle*, it has been my eternal pleasure. Please scold my brother for keeping you hidden away for himself."

I scowled, Katya laughed, and my sister was

"She is everything they say." Katya rearranged herself on the *chaise longue*, folding her hands in her lap and tossing out her dark curls upon the arm.

My scowl only deepened. "Please retain your former pose." I looked at my drawing. It was terrible, the angle of the face all wrong. Anger rose in my throat like bile. With a curse, I tore it from the book and hurled it, crumpled, into the corner. Katya raised an eyebrow in a look hovering between sympathy and amusement. Taking up my pencil, and struggling to contain my ill humour, I started afresh.

We attended Gabrielle's *vernissage*, of course, her latest collection (themed around classical nature spirits – dryads, nymphs, hamadryads and the like – but relocated to sophisticated modern environments to save it from being *passé*) held in Madame Bouvier's new gallery off *Chemin du Carrat*. Ironically, this was but a stone's throw from the cafe where I first met Katya. A momentary suspicion that this was a deliberate *provocation* on the part of my sister afflicted me, but I dismissed it. I told myself that not everything Gabrielle did was designed to infuriate me. It was a large and upcoming *galerie*, a haunt of the fashionable, and the exposure to both our benefit. I did my duty, drinking the finest champagne, touring the installations with Katya on my arm. We stayed for an hour or two, then exited into the early evening drizzle. Truly, the work was remarkable, but Gabrielle and I had an unspoken agreement that unless mounting a joint *exposition* we would not detract attention from the other's shows. I stayed long enough that the tongues of the envious would not wag, attempting to divine the degree of my approval in the time that I spent, then left her to the plaudits of the elite. Katya had taken an apartment in Villeneuve and we parted there, I hurrying back across the river to continue working on what I hoped would be my *chef d'oeuvre*, a nude in marble of Katya as Proserpine, caught in the moment of Hades' seizing, for which I was producing a series of studies in clay. If it were right, if she breathed in this, then her part in the Great Work would be assured.

I worked all that night, and throughout the next day, drawing passion, grief, turmoil of the heart from mute clay. In each, I sought to uncover *la vérité du moment*, the true expression of darkness, fear, terror of her assault, and yet still the light and wonder she brought to the underworld. How to encapsulate that in one expression, in one outstretched arm, rejecting and embracing. In this there could be no repeat of my Alexander, no inhuman torque of muscle and flesh. Each study drew me further into the soul of the piece and took me further from the malaise I had fallen into. In Katya I had found perfection. She was inhabited by that divine spirit that engenders genius with inspiration. She was a sun, and like all celestial beings she drew lesser bodies into her orbit, to circle helplessly until that day they expired, immolated.

Each day I would meet her, outside the palace, by the river, or in a shaded courtyard. We sat, drinking thick sweet *kahvesi* at the Turkish café, after which Katya would upend our cups, laughing, and pretend to tell our fortunes in the method her grandmother had taught her. At one such reading I sat, glowering, as she foretold that our paths would diverge, and only the heartache of the rejected suitor would remain. *Sébastien*, she said, with a mischievous smile, *I see that you will tire of me. My beauty will fail as these sere leaves wither and fail.* With a fingertip she turned my face towards the other diners. *Are there no other beauties to entrance your eye?* I shook her hand away, and she, seeing that I was discomfited by her gentle mockery, made light of it, calling for more coffee and offering a different reading in which I was elevated to the finest artist of the coming century. But I had felt something cold touch me, even then, and she did no more readings after that.

On other days we would walk, arm in arm, through the dappled lawns of the *Rocher des Doms*, high above the winding streets. Everywhere I would draw, seeking to capture each expression she was capable of, the hint of the ineffable, the great illusion of mortality behind which my eternal goddess hid. Once, I allowed her to be captured by a street photographer who (to her secret delight) pestered us incessantly until I acquiesced. Reluctant as I was to permit a mere *flâneur,* an itinerant observer of the common herd, to possess her in any way, I was equally determined to see whether the lens could capture something the eye could not. I had long been sceptical of the idea that a mere contrivance of silver and glass might effect some transformative expression, but after long arguments with Gabrielle, had conceded that such a device might offer a new expression of the Laronde genius. The following day we hurried to the photographer's studio on *Rue Paillasserie,* where Katya engaged Monsieur Cancienne in conversation whilst I feverishly searched his prints. They were fascinating. Enticing, yet aloof. Alive, yet two dimensional. Unquestionably, Katya herself stared at me from them, yet they could not contain her. Still she revealed only what she might. The lens was an inquisitor, relentless, but it had driven her light underground. Some, however, were more revealing, capturing an intensity I had omitted, and I resolved to investigate the process further. Katya was, of course, delighted with the prints that I purchased for her. I ordered another set to be delivered to our house, and we stepped back out into the Vaucluse sunlight.

It was a month before I began the sculpture; a fortnight merely to choose the marble. I procrastinated, made decisions only to change them when the stone was delivered, and drove the suppliers to near distraction. In the end, there really was no choice, only the best could be considered, the finest *puro bianco* from the Italian quarries. This would offer me the most beautiful polish – a shimmering white, translucent as skin, the pale purity of the tormented goddess. This would be my medium. Katya stood in my studio, surrounded by sketches, clay studies of her face, limbs, the folds of her gown, its hem, the tiniest details of her hair. I wanted to show her the timeless, immortal stone that would capture her. I wanted her to see the raw block, how it would be cut and chiselled and polished to expose the marvel inside, and, in so doing, ultimately reveal that which was her divine form, rather than the transient mortal frame that concealed her. I spoke as I arranged my tools – the hammers, the flat and fork chisels of a dozen different sizes, sandpapers, pumice. Everything I would need.

"The origins of this are lost." I touched the stone lovingly. "Not the stone, that is as old as the earth." I looked at her as she raised her eyebrows, noting how expressive the narrowing of the forehead made her seem. "The word itself, such a word that is as smooth and beautiful as the stone it describes. Marble. Every European language takes the Greek as its root, from *marmaros,* 'the shining stone.' So beautiful." I smiled. "Yet it isn't even a Greek word, it goes far, far back. A line, a circle that has yet to reach its conclusion. And for you, I have chosen the purest of all . . . this has no imperfections, no sand or iron or serpentine to traduce the purity, to adulterate the fire of its inception."

Katya looked at the unhewn block. "It looks so much less . . . than what it will become."

I spread my hand upon the block. It was rough; I sensed the grain beneath my skin. "And yet it sings to me." I pressed my ear to the ridges, to the irregularity from which I would coax perfection. "Truly, it sings. Inside, it waits." I looked up, and smiled. "Marble is the only stone that knows what it is to be human."

Katya leaned forward in her seat, her hands clutching her knees. Her eyes flashed. "Yes! Yes! Tell me, what do you see? What do you hear?" She crossed the studio in two strides, and seized my arm. "It is for this I came to you. This genius!" Her hands touched my face, her fingers tracing the line of my eyes. "No-one sees like you, like Laronde! It is as if you see within the stone, the contours of a soul that is deep inside. What do you see there? Tell me, what does it say?"

I grabbed her hands, her fingers long and pale as bone. Gently I kissed their warm tips, misted her nails with my breath. Then I held them to my chest. "Inside. It is not enough to see the stone, to trade blows with its obstinacy. It will harbour its secrets, it will resist the metamorphosis it must make." Her eyes, wide and black as the shadows under the papal arch, stared into mine. "To truly know, to coax the figure, the skin into the light, to mould that shining stone into the translucency of beauty, ah then one must go within. One must travel deep into the rock. *Become* its experience, hear the beating of its heart. Dwell within it, learn what it has seen, what immemorial forces have twisted it, shaped it, and even now lie frozen, waiting to burst forth beneath the artist's hand and for one glorious moment of dust and light, to be seized, and then . . . then, if the artist is worthy of the gift, to be fixed for all time looking out. Revealed." Katya was immobile, enthralled. I place her hand against the marble. "This is Laronde. This is our gift. To travel to that place all art dwells, the still point of the Universe that is the mind of our Mother, and bring back what we find."

She breathed out. A long ecstatic sigh. "Art made flesh," she whispered. I kissed her. I had found my goddess.

○

Ours is not a common gift. What might take lesser hands years of work could be achieved in half or less due to our unique kinship with the stone. In three months, I had summoned form from within the implacable rock. In six, Proserpine stretched her hand longingly upwards, her eyes yearning for the fragrant woods of summer even as her expression hardened into despair. Her gown, strewn with petals torn from the clutching stems of lupine and primrose, swirled in folds about her slender legs even as the earth yawned and the dark fields of Tartaros yawed empty beneath. In twelve months, she was caught, snared by the sorrowful King as surely as I had snared the latent harvest of my peerless stone and set it, with all the fire of the living muse, before the world's adoring gaze. Even Bernini's *Rape of Proserpina* would yield before Laronde. No doubt assailed me. I worked in a fever of certainty.

Gabrielle visited often. Of my sister, I would concede that she was not cruel, but rather possessed of an honesty that was often mistaken for such. For that reason, she was as generous with praise as she was with criticism. Sometimes she stood for hours watching me toil, as motionless as the stone I inhabited, only a nod or quick word to indicate her approval. As winter drove the last of the brown autumn leaves from the plane trees of the cobbled squares, and luminous sunsets gave way to the grey shrouds of the mistral's attendants, she would examine my *Proserpine Seized* minutely, her lips parting in whispered words I could not hear. Nor did she neglect her own work, for I knew that acclaim for her collection had elevated her to the foremost of our generation, and she was increasingly absent, a viewing in Paris here, an installation in Milan there. Always she would return, appearing in my studio amid the dappling and shifting light, her gown a patchwork of blues and golds in the strange and dreamlike undertones of our gallery. Her silence was praise enough. Once only she addressed me directly. She cupped the face of Proserpine in one hand, caressing the smooth pale stone, so lifelike in appearance but cool beyond human experience. "*C'est votre chef d'oeuvre.*" she murmured. "Your masterpiece."

Sometimes Katya was present, rapt. The stage of preparation, of modelling, was long past, but I found her presence focused me, bound us to the stone. Hours would pass in silence, and sometimes she would leave to wander our galleries or workshops, only to return at the end of the day and find me still carving, still smoothing the alabaster skin, each touch an affirmation. At her urging, I would leave my tools and go back into the sun or moonlight (for I lost track of time), and while away a few precious hours in a bar or restaurant before impatience drove me back to the stone. To finish was all I desired.

There came a late winter's day when I emerged of my own volition. I had reached for a finishing claw, and remembered that I had discarded my favoured four-point the previous year, having worn it beyond use. With increasing desperation I scrabbled through boxes of chisels, upending several in my quest, and even considered raiding Gabrielle's. I paused outside her attic workshop where I knew she kept her smaller pieces, but something held me back. We did not meddle with each other's tools, they were extensions of our will and moulded to our hands. With reluctance (I had been working in a feverish state for a good thirty hours without break) I drew on a topcoat (more for appearance than necessity) and hurried into the chill street. It was early evening, but I knew Monsieur Fernsby would open his shop for me. Clouds hung swollen, their urgent bellies promising a tempest. Whether of snow or rain I was uncaring and oblivious, rehearsing in my head the precise strokes that would reveal my figure's hand, clutching to preserve her modesty as her gown was torn away. I purchased the chisel as swiftly as I could, thrusting thrice the value into the Englishman's hand, and waved away his proffered change. He smiled as he locked the doors behind me, having long experience with myself and Gabrielle's manic whims. I hurried back along the street, shops fronting the implacable mediaeval wall, and turned into the *Passage de l'Oratoire*, a narrow cut that would lead me back to the Papal

Palace and our own *maison*. As I hastened through a small, cobbled courtyard, my eye was caught by a wayside gallery, half hidden by the twisted boughs of a sickly fir. Something in the window beyond the shuttered yard arrested me. Quickly, I rattled the door onto the street, which I found to be firmly barred. With a glance at the deserted street, I scaled the railings and dropped into the yard, then, cupping my face in my hands, I pressed my nose against the freezing glass. There could be no mistake.

Two portraits of Katya hung in the shop.

In one, she had been captured at a cafe in the square, smiling, twisting the pendants of her emerald necklace. Its filigree caught the sunlight, and reflected in the long-stemmed glass in her other hand. She wore a gown I had bought her. The other . . .

Stepping back, I wrenched the door from its frame. Brick dust and splinters exploded around me. I crossed to the painting. She was reclining, face thoughtful. She gazed beyond the artist, hand lifting a stray strand of hair from eyes that were lit by the moonlight that fell into Gabrielle's attic studio. She wore nothing at all.

Fury consumed me. Something primordial awoke as I stared, transfixed at the cool mystery of Katya's smile, the silver sheen on her naked breasts. I tore the canvas from its frame and drew back my fist. I hesitated. In all the years of our collaboration, it was implicit that we never tampered with each other's art, no matter how defective or inferior. Art contains us, a fragment of our will, and to take it upon ourselves to do so would be to consume the other's experience. It was forbidden.

With a bellow of anguish, I smashed my fist through the canvas. I shredded it, ripping the smile, the face of my goddess, into a hundred pieces, wrenching the limbs that had woven their pale seduction upon me from the body. If there had been a heart, I would have torn that too from the canvas. Then, hurling the defiled ruins of my sister's betrayal across the gallery, I kicked and tore my way through the mockery that every painting, every portrait and wan, simpering smile offered me, and burst into the street.

I ran, I ran through the empty, locked streets, bars and shutters of a world that cared nothing for the gift that I had brought them, for the art or purpose I had given my life to. By the cobbles and markets where Katya and I had walked, arm in arm, talking of painting, music, history, by the coffee houses and theatres where I had sketched and captured her every mood. Back to the mansion of our hopes, where Gabrielle had spun her elaborate games and I, oblivious, had planned that Katya would be my greatest inspiration.

I threw myself against the doors. They smashed apart in a riot of crumbling timbers as I took the stairs two at a time. I knew where the portrait had been painted. Gabrielle's attic, among the empty and shrouded apartments of occasional guests, where she maintained a lesser studio, entranced by the light of a natural sky. A pit yawned in my stomach as I realised my sister and Katya may have been within even as I considered searching for a chisel a bare half-hour since.

"Open!" I bellowed, hammering at the door. "Katya!"

I kicked the door from its hinges, stumbling across the threshold into the cramped room, throwing wood and easels aside. A lamp burned under the ceiling, and the embers of a fire glowed in the grate, but there was no sign of my sister or Katya. A faint scent of jasmine hung in the air, mingling with the elusive myrrh and rose of Katya's own Parisian fragrance. Bile rose in my throat. It was fresh; they had been here within the hour. But where now?

My stomach yawed like a pit. La Ronde. Surely my sister had not taken Katya to our most sacred place? Stolen the privilege that I had laboured and planned for?

I ran down the stairs, back through the corridors and catacombs of our home, along the still, echoing hallways, past the rooms crammed with canvases and statues, bronzes, tapestries, murals, mosaics, spiral staircases hung with portraits and busts, the great and good, the fair and foul. The grand visions of a hundred generations, invisible to me. I had thought only for Katya, for Gabrielle, and for La Ronde.

I skidded to a halt before the jewelled doors of our great circle, breathing deeply to slow the agony in my chest, dispel the cloud before my eyes. A vice wrung pity from my heart's chambers, turning it to dust as dry as the desert wind. I raised my hands, willed their shaking to cease. I must be calm to be that art that comes at life's end.

I threw open the doors. Beyond, lamps glowed ceaselessly upon the marvel of our race, faces drawn in silent consternation. Whispers held the air aloft, trapped with the breath of angels beneath the immaculate canopy of gold. Gabrielle and Katya stood, fittingly, before our father's likeness. All I had eyes for were their hands, fingers white as porcelain entwined, joining them. My face became blind Justice, the unanswerable giver of fate, stern and chastising. My footsteps rang upon the red mosaic.

Gabrielle turned, quicker than Katya, eyes wide as she realised she had been discovered. Emotions flashed across her face, rose and fell like empires. Triumph, glee, pride, pity . . . and then the wide-eyes of fear as she saw my intent, that my passion, my creation, would not be brooked.

"*Sébastien!*" she cried. "*C'est impossible! Not now!*" I brushed her aside, and fell upon Katya.

As I separated her flesh, layer by layer undid her muscles and sought our truth within the cage of white that was her inmost beauty, as her eyes glazed with a kind of rapture and I beheld the purity of her extremity, I savoured then what my father savoured. For the first time I felt close to him, to the world of his hands and the ministries of his talent. I knew what his love had made possible, the depths of his joy uncovered as our mother became his fondest pupil, together enshrined in the oneness of his art. So I laboured, as he had laboured to usher us forth into light from the marvellous skin of stone that shone around us, that red stone that could only be irrigated by the immutable sacrifice of the flesh. I fed the ropes of Katya's body through my hands, rough cords alive in their sinew as her body rose and fell like a tempest-tossed vessel straining against its lines, desiring to be free, and her wordless cry spiralled and spiralled into inarticulacy high in the painted dome. Her blood to water them, and my passion to pull upon them as if to raise a sail against a storm of desire and her soliloquies of pain. And when at last she lay, piece by piece exposed in the divinity of her composition, so La Ronde bestowed its miracle, merging our fire and beauty into the living sculpture of our child, hewn from stone and blood. Thus did I become my father, raising up my son from this flooded pasture, and I knew it would be my child that carried La Ronde into the future, not Gabrielle's.

○

I am blind now. Gabrielle chiselled out my eyes
even as I ascended to my place in the Great Work,
beside our father. Before she did so, her own olive
eyes wet with tears, she stood with one hand upon
the head of my son, and her face bore no expression
I could read. The cloth in her other dripped with
the scarlet she had wiped from his shivering body,
the final gift of my shrieking muse. I had been
victorious, yet it would be Gabrielle who would
go on, from whom my son would learn. The *tap
tap* of her hammer, the edge of her chisel against
the marble of my cheek, her whispers in my ear,
would be the last manifestation of the realm of
my senses. Even as the living presence of the stone
filled my hollow veins with its beat, and I hung
like Prometheus, rent by savage claws for his gift
to humanity, her words became our coda.

"*Be broken and pure, mon petit frère. Be broken
and pure.*"

www.ingramcontent.com/pod-product-compliance
Lightning Source LLC
Chambersburg PA
CBHW030652190726
48286CB00008B/2780